Lisa's Testimony

To Dave + Jackie —
Be blessed

Terri Blaxell-Wayson

1

A dog's walk through the 23rd Psalm

By Terri Blazell-Wayson

~

Her name is Lisa.
She is ten years old
and she weighs 9 ½ pounds.
She is a min-pin – a miniature pinscher.

What can we learn from a little dog
about the love of God
and those mystifying times
when we don't always see or understand
what He is doing?

We can learn so very much.

Here is her story "in her own words".

~

~

Psalm 23:1-3

The LORD is my shepherd;
I shall not want.
He makes me to lie down in green pastures;
He leads me beside the still waters.
He restores my soul.

~

~

My master takes very good care of me.
I have no wants.
She gives me cool water to drink
and lets me lie down in the green grass.
She gives me belly rubs
which fills my soul with such joy.

~

~

My name is Lisa.

I am a believer in the great Master Creator.

The very first book of the Bible,
tells us that the Master Creator
breathed His breath of Life
into all living creatures.

Did you know that it is the same breath of Life[1]
that He breathed into the first human being?

That is something
all God's creatures have in common -
the breath of Life from the Master Creator.

~

---

[1] Genesis 1:30 and 2:7

~

I'm adopted.

I don't remember much
about my birth family.

I remember that it was soft
and warm
and crowded.

I remember the sweet taste
of mama's milk.

The squirming, fuzzy bodies
of my brothers and sisters.

~

~

I do remember the day
my master took me home.
I fit in the palm of her hand.

She covered me with her other hand,
held me close to her face
and spoke softly and tenderly to me.

She placed me on her neck,
covered me with the collar of her jacket
and that's how we drove home.

~

~

That night she put me in a box
with a soft, warm blanket
and put it under the kitchen table.
It was dark and I was so alone.
I began to whimper.

My master came for me.
She carried me to her bed
and told me that I could stay there
just for the night
until I got used to my new home.
I found the perfect place to sleep,
curled into a little ball in the crook
at the back of her knees.

Ten years later
I'm still sleeping there.

~

~

Psalm 23: 3

He leads me in the paths of righteousness
For His name's sake.

~

~

My master holds my leash
and leads me along the paths that I should go.

~

~

One day,
when I was just a few months old,
my master took me
for a car ride.

I LOVE car rides!

We didn't go very far.
When we got out of the car,
there were so many new smells
all around,
on the sidewalk,
in the grass.
Lots of other dog smells.

What an exciting place!

~

~

But then, she took me through a door
into a building

and everything changed.

I could smell
fear and pain and death
all around me.

I could smell
chemicals,
metal,
disinfectant
and strangers.

I did not like this place.

~

~

I turned and tried to run out the door
but my master held tight to my leash.

I did not know what
my master had to do there
but I hoped that we would leave soon.

I heard her tell the stranger,
"We have an appointment" and
"Yes, she's six months old."

And I knew they were talking about me.
But I didn't know what it meant.

~

~

To my horror, she bent down
and picked me up.
She handed me across
the stainless steel counter
to the stranger.

Even though the stranger spoke kindly to me
I strained to get out of her arms and
back to my master.

But she held me tight and took me away.

Surely my master will reach for me.
Surely she won't let this stranger take me away.

But she did.

~

~

The stranger carried me farther and farther
away from my master.
She took me into another room
and closed the door.
Other strangers came.
They looked into my ears, my eyes, my mouth.
They poked me with sharp things.

I cried.

~

~

Why did my master do this?
I thought she loved me.
Will my master come back for me?
Will I ever see her again?

What did I do wrong?

~

~

The strangers put me in a cage.
I was utterly alone.
All I could do was
lay my head on my paws and cry.
Later one of the strangers
took me out of the cage.

Had my master come back for me?

~

~

Instead, she laid me on a table and
poked me with a sharp thing again.
Everything started to go dark.
I couldn't move.
I thought I was dying.

My master brought me here to die.

I must have done something really bad
for my master to want me to die.

~

~

I don't know how long
I was in the dark place.

I woke up and realized
that I was not dead
but something was terribly wrong.

I was back in my cage, I hurt terribly and
I could tell that the strangers had done
something to me.
I hurt along my belly down by my back legs.
I tried to look but they had put a large plastic
thing around my neck.

I heard voices but
none of them were my master.

~

~

They brought me food and water.
I did not want anything.
This was my home now; all alone in a small
cage, horrible things being done to me.
Pain. Sadness. Abandonment.

I wanted to die.

Job 17:11-12 [NIV]

My days have passed, my plans are shattered.
Yet the desires of my heart
turn night into day;
in the face of the darkness light is near.

I prayed my master would come back for me.

~

~

I don't know how long I was there.
It might have been years.

They kept checking on me
and poking me.
Then they picked me up
and carried me away.

Were they going to do more bad things to me?

Instead, there was my master!

~

~

They put me in her arms and
she snuggled me
as best she could and
talked kindly to me.

I was so happy to see her but
I was afraid and confused, too.

Was she going to leave me again?
Would more bad things happen?

My master carried me gently to her car,
away from that horrible place
and took me home.

~

~

It was a long time before she took
that plastic thing off of my neck.
The first thing I did was look at my belly.
There was a long horrible scar on it.
I touched it with my nose.

I felt a pain but
it wasn't coming from my wound.
It was coming from my heart.
I looked at my master.
My eyes were sad.
I don't know why she let this happen to me.

Didn't she love me?

~

~

There is a verse in my master's Bible that says,

"And we know that all things
work together for good
to those who love God."[2]

I decided that even though
I didn't understand what happened,
my master loves me so much,
that even something that
seems bad to me,
must be good for me.

~

---

[2] Romans 8:28a

~

I've never seen them
but my master has scars, too.

I know,
because sometimes
I see her on her knees…
and she is crying.

And I know. I just know.

~

~

The wounds heal but the scars remain.

~

~

But my master and I are not alone.

Our great Master Creator
knows all about scars.
He sent His Son to this earth
to show us His love.

Instead,
they bloodied His back
with whips,
they nailed him to a cross,
they stuck a crown of thorns
into His head and
they cut His side with a spear.

~

~

The Great Master Creator
knows all about wounds and scars.

"But He was wounded
for our transgressions,
He was bruised for our iniquities;
the chastisement for our peace
was upon Him, and by His stripes
we are healed."[3]

Someday, He will heal us of our scars
but His will never go away.

~

---

[3] Isaiah 53:5

~

Psalm 23:4

Yea, though I walk through the valley
of the shadow of death,
I will fear no evil;
For You are with me;
Your rod and Your staff,
they comfort me.

~

~

There are places
no one wants to go to.
There are things
no one wants to face.
But my master goes with me
and I am safe.
Her hand holding my leash
comforts me.

~

~

One day, not too long ago,
we went for a long walk.

I LOVE walks.

We were out for quite awhile when
the sky grew dark and it began to rain.
Not a little rain but a lot.
The drops were hard and heavy
and very cold like needles of ice.
I tried to turn back and go home.

But my master kept pulling me the other way.

~

~

I fought her by pulling hard
against my leash.
But we kept going my master's way,
farther from the warmth and comfort of home.

I was afraid and once again it seemed
as though my master didn't care about me.
We ran through the pouring rain and abruptly,
my master turned into a grove of trees.

We had never gone this way before.

~

~

The trees closed in over our heads.
It sheltered us from the rain
but the path through them was dark and dense,
like a valley of shadows before us.
I could smell deer and coyotes
and raccoons and possums.
All things that could kill me -
could kill us.

This place smelled like death.

~

~

What was wrong with my master?
Why would she bring me into this place?
Why didn't we go back home the way I wanted
to go? Instead, she brought me into this
dark, strange, dangerous place.

This valley of shadows and death.

~

~

My master bent down and picked me up.
She placed me inside her coat
and we hurried along.
She kept whispering in soothing tones but
fear kept me from understanding her voice.

I'm sure she wanted me to trust her
but I still did not feel safe.
If only my master had listened to me
and gone back home the way I wanted to go.
Now we were lost in this frightening place.

~

~

Just like before,
when she left me with those strangers,
my master was letting me down.

I could not understand her actions
so they must be wrong.
She wasn't doing things the way
I thought would be best.

~

~

Then, as quickly as we had entered
the valley of shadows and death,
we came out the other side
through a break in the trees.

It was still raining hard but
when she set me down on the sidewalk,
I knew where we were!
We were only a short way from home.

~

~

If we had gone back the way
I had wanted to,
we would have been out for
a very long time.

We would have gotten
very wet and very cold.

But my master knew the better way.

~

~

My master wrote a poem about
her Master Creator that explains it best.
A line in it goes like this:

... the most dangerous place
If held within Your hands
is the most safest place...[4]

~

---

[4] There Are Times [pages 70-71]

~

Every once in awhile,
I push my nose against that scar on my belly
and I still wonder what it was all about.

But I not only trust my master;
I trust her Creator and mine.

~

~

Psalm 23:5-6
You prepare a table before me
in the presence of my enemies.
You anoint my head with oil;
My cup runs over.

~

~

She prepares delicious food and
sets it before me.
The cats are not allowed to touch it.
She rubs my fur with oil
to keep it moist and prevent fleas.
I am overwhelmed by her love and care.

~

~

"Are not five sparrows sold for two pennies?
Yet not one of them is forgotten by God.
Indeed, the very hairs of your head
are all numbered." [5]

Jesus said that.

~

---

[5] Luke 12:6-7 [NIV]

~

That means a lot to me.
You see, I'm a shedder!
I leave hair everywhere.
Just ask my master!

But what that verse is really saying is
our Master Creator knows
each one of us so intimately,
that each time a single hair falls
He takes another inventory.

He's paying that close of attention.

~

~

The rest of that verse goes on to say,

"Don't be afraid; you are worth more
than many sparrows."

- and many min-pins.

You see, you are so valuable to Him that
He died on a cross for you.

In other words,
He'd rather die than live without you.

~

~

He knows the number of
hairs on your head
at any moment in time.

He knows all about your
wounds and scars –
every last detail.

That is how much He loves you.

~

~

Psalm 23:6

Surely goodness and mercy shall follow me
All the days of my life;
And I will dwell in the
house of the LORD
Forever.

~

~

My master's unconditional love
has followed me all my life.
Her home is my home always.

~

~

My master is 357 years old now
- in dog years-
but there are things in her life that
she still doesn't understand.
She has to wait until
she meets with her Master Creator and
He explains it all to her
just like me.

~

~

There is a song she listens to
that explains it best.

It goes like this:

"God is too wise to be mistaken.
God is too good to be unkind.
So when you don't understand,
when you can't trace His hand,
when you can't see His plan,
trust His heart."[6]

~

---

[6] "Trust His Heart" Words and Music by Eddie Carswell and Babbie Mason

~

Sometimes
my master cries.

Sometimes
she is scared.

Sometimes
she is sad but

I know from her prayers
that she trusts the heart
of her Master Creator.

~

~

And I also see His
love,
peace and
joy
in her heart
through all the storms
that life brings.

~

~

I'm ten years old now.
That's old for a dog.

I don't know
how many more years I have left.

A little boy put it best.
He said,

"Everybody is born so that
they can learn to live a good life –
like loving everybody and being nice.
Well, dogs already know how to do that,
so they don't have to stay on this earth as long."[7]

~

---

[7] Source unknown.

~

However long we have,
life is short.

If you don't know
the love and forgiveness
of the Master Creator,
ask Him now.

He will begin to heal
the wounds that are still raw
and erase the scars that are still visible.

~

~

When I stand in the presence of
the great Master Creator,
I will ask Him about that
scar on my belly
and He will tell me.

No matter what He says,
I know that it is there because
my earthly master meant it for my good
even if I could not understand it on this earth.

~

~

It's the same for my master and her scars.
She knows that her Master Creator
loves her and that she has always
been in His hands in spite of the scars
and through all her
valleys of shadows and death.

So give your heart to the
loving Master Creator and
the Savior who
gave His all for you –
the One who has meant
all things
for good and will
never ever leave you.

~

~

It would be my greatest reward
if one day after you've
passed through
the valley of shadows and death
to find that you are
Home
on the other side
and you knelt before
the Master Creator and said,

"I am here because of Lisa's testimony."

~

~

Now, there are some things
that my master has taught me and
they are the same things that
the great Master Creator is teaching her.
I know that I am a happier dog
when I obey them.

Here are the main four:

~

~

Come
Come to me all who are weary and burdened,
and I will give you rest. Matthew 11:28 [NIV]

Sit
Sit at my feet and learn from me for I am gentle
and humble in heart. Matthew 11:29
[In my master's words]

~

~

Stay
For I will never leave you nor forsake you.
Hebrews 13:5b

And Fetch!
Go into all the world and tell everyone that the
Master Creator loves them. Mark 16:15.
[In my master's words]

~

~

Epilogue:
[From Lisa's master]

Four years after Lisa "shared her testimony",
she was diagnosed with advanced
congestive heart failure.
She was put on medication and
did very well for many months.
[Longer than many dogs do
with that kind of diagnosis.]

On the night of February 9,
I took her out for her evening walk.
She stepped out of her harness which was
deliberately left loose
so as not to put pressure on her chest.

~

~

I stood there and watched her walk slowly
through the snow and back behind the bushes
where ordinarily her leash would not
allow her to go.

I remember thinking,
She's been on a leash her whole life,
let her be free just this once.

The night was cool and still and beautiful and
I sensed that there was something special
about this silent, snowy night.
Early the next morning on February 10, 2014
Lisa collapsed and never regained
consciousness.
She stepped into eternity
and met our precious Master Creator.

~

~

In her lifetime,
Lisa lived in or visited seven states.
She flew on a plane.
She appeared on the cover of a brochure
and in a magazine.
She was an avid hiker and hiked
all over Western Washington.

She was a therapy dog and volunteered
at a nursing home in the memory care unit
where she sat on patient's laps.

~

~

I imagine her sitting on God's lap
as he scratches her ears
and they are both looking down on me.
When she sees my tears or
senses my fear,
she whispers
Don't be afraid.
It is only temporary.
Remember,
The Valley of shadows and death
Is a shortcut.
And just like you never left me,
The Master Creator will never leave you.

~

~

Lisa's testimony
has been shared at
Celebrate Recovery
and other church groups.
Even years later,
people come up to me and
tell me how much
her testimony meant to them.

~

~

I hope her story has touched you, too.
And in your deepest, darkest moments
that you will remember
how much Jesus loves you
and you are not alone.

~

[This is the master's poem that Lisa quotes from on page 42]

~

There are Times
By Terri Blazell-Wayson

There are those times
When it is completely in Your hands
and we know it.

We try to act brave
And say we will not be afraid
but we show it.

We know our ocean is calm
In the deep,
the storm can only sway the top.

But we live in the boat
So we cry,
"make it stop!"

But there are times
When it is completely in Your hands
and we know it.

There are those times
When we are plunged so far beneath the deep
we cannot breathe.

We know we shouldn't thrash about
Or fight it; only collapse within Your hands
and believe

That the most dangerous place
If held within Your hands
is the most safest place...

For there are times
When it is completely in your hands
and we know it.

~

~

Lisa's Psalm

My master takes very good care of me.
I have no wants.
She gives me cool water to drink
and lets me lie down in the green grass.
She gives me belly rubs
which fills my soul with such joy.

My master holds my leash
and leads me
along the paths that I should go.

There are places no one wants to go to.
There are things no one wants to face.
But my master goes with me
and I am safe.

Her hand holding my leash
comforts me.
She prepares delicious food and
sets it before me.
The cats are not allowed to touch it.

She rubs my fur with oil
to keep it moist and prevent fleas.

I am overwhelmed by her love and care.

My master's unconditional love
has followed me all my life.
Her home is my home always.

~

I Have Known Angels
By Terri Blazell-Wayson

I have known angels.
Four-legged furry ones
Who lick my face each morning
And leap joyously
into my arms every night.
No questions asked.
No judgments made.
Just glad I'm there.

I have known angels
That lay quiet in my lap
When I am lonely
When I am sad
When I am afraid
And without saying a word
I know
That they know
The deepest ache of my heart.

I have known angels
With a wet nose for wings
A wagging tail for a halo
And fur for celestial robes
Who leap instead of fly
And bark instead of sing.
And still, they stand guardian
Over my being
As well as my soul.

I have held angels
in my arms as they breathed
their last earthly breath
and wept with a grief so great
I thought my heart
would never recover,
Grieving that
they were going Home
Yet grateful that of all the people on earth
God chose to send them to me.

~

Made in the
USA
Monee, IL